iT'S SHOW-TIME,
ELViS!

In memory of Sarah - N.S.

First published 2006 by Macmillan Children's Books
This edition published 2006 by Macmillan Children's Books
a division of Macmillan Publishers Limited
20 New Wharf Road, London N1 9RR
Basingstoke and Oxford
Associated companies throughout the world
www.panmacmillan.com

ISBN-13: 978-1-4050-5328-0
ISBN-10: 1-4050-5328-3

Text copyright © Andrew Murray 2006
Illustrations copyright © Nicola Slater 2006
Moral rights asserted.

35798642

A CIP catalogue record for this book is available from the British Library.

Printed in Belgium by Proost

ANDREW MURRAY

IT'S SHOW-TIME, ELVIS!

Illustrated by
NICOLA SLATER

MACMILLAN CHILDREN'S BOOKS

Buddy the dog was

ALWAYS HAPPY.

So eager to please, so eager to help. Always rolling over, begging and wagging his tail . . .

"You're such a GOOD boy!" fussed Lucy.

"You're such a PAIN!" scowled Elvis.

One day, Lucy saw a poster.

DOG SHOW

Is your dog happy? Friendly?
Bright-eyed and waggy-tailed?

If so, why not enter your
four-legged friend in the

Happiest Dog
Competition

at this year's Dog Show?

"Oh, Buddy!" cried Lucy.
"Who's the friendliest dog?"

"I AM!"

"Who's the
waggiest dog?"

"I AM!"

"Who's the happiest dog?"

"I AM!"

Elvis groaned.
"Who's the most
annoying dog?"

"YOU ARE . . ."

On the day of the dog show, Lucy was getting ready to go.

"Come on, Buddy!"

"Hurry up!" said Lucy.
"I've packed everything,
including your favourite treats."

"OH NO,
YOU HAVEN'T!"
grinned Elvis...

as he pulled out the doggy treats . . .
and pushed in some kipper snacks.
"That will take the wag out of his tail!" he thought.

At that moment, Buddy came in, so Elvis hid.
"Let's go," said Lucy, picking up her bag.
"IT'S SHOW-TIME!"

"This is it, Buddy!"
said Lucy,

throwing him a doggy treat to make him . . .

SUPER WAGGY.

Only it wasn't a doggy treat.
"YUCK!" said Buddy.

And as he chewed . . .

his tail flopped.

His ears dropped.

And his tongue popped out.

The judge wasn't impressed.

"What's the matter, Buddy?" whispered Lucy.
Elvis knew.

With a paper cup . . .

little doggy socks . . .

and a doggy jacket . . .

there stood
ELViS –
the strangest dog
you've ever seen!

He took a deep breath, and stepped into the show-ring.

DOGS, DOGS —
SO MANY DOGS!

And just one cat – a frightened cat.

"PSST!" whispered Elvis.
"Buddy, I've brought you a real dog treat.
I swapped them with my kipper snacks."

"I'm so sorry.
Please cheer up."

Buddy looked up slowly.

"ELViS! If these dogs find out you're a cat, YOU'LL be a dog treat!"

Elvis turned around.

All the dogs
were staring.
All their tails had
stopped wagging.

Elvis needed
to fit in . . . and

FAST!

He rolled over.

He begged.

He wagged
his tail.

He had the
lickiest tongue . . .

the tickliest tummy . . .

and the waggiest tail of all
the dogs in the show-ring.

"WE HAVE A WINNER!"

the judge declared.

"I've never seen a dog so …

STRANGE.

But I've never seen a dog so happy!"

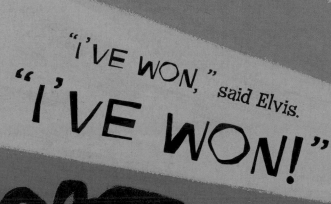

"I'VE WON," said Elvis.
"I'VE WON!"

Proudly, he held his doggy nose high . . .

waggled his doggy ears . . .

"CAT!" growled the dogs.

"He's making fools of us! GET HIM!"

The dogs charged . . .

and Lucy RAN –
with Elvis in her bag.

But Buddy didn't move.

"LEAVE MY FRIENDS ALONE!" he snarled.

And, no matter how big, strong or fierce . . .

NO dog was braver than Buddy!

Back home, Buddy and Elvis found themselves alone.
Lucy had been gone for ages.
Then they saw the poster on her door.

Elvis gave Buddy a little shove.

"Go on, Buddy! You deserve the prize this time!"

So Buddy opened the door, and . . .

"HERE ARE THE WINNERS!"
Lucy announced,
presenting them BOTH with
trophies and treats.

1st

1st

Elvis's whiskers quivered with excitement.
And Buddy's tail just WAG-WAG-WAGGED!